The Falling Flowers

By Jennifer B. Reed
Illustrations by Dick Cole

Library of Congress Cataloging-in-Publication Data

Reed, Jennifer.
    The falling flowers / by Jennifer B. Reed ; illustrated by Dick Cole.
        p. cm.
    Summary: Mayumie and her grandmother take a trip into Tokyo to see a
surprise even more fun than the zoo and more beautiful than the shrine:
cherry blossoms flowering in the heart of the city.
    ISBN 1-885008-28-7
    [1. Grandmothers--Fiction. 2. Japanese flowering cherry--Fiction. 3.
Trees--Fiction. 4. Tokyo (Japan)--Fiction. 5. Japan--Fiction.] I. Cole,
Dick, ill. II. Title.

PZ7.R25235Fal 2005
[E]--dc22

2005017979

To two wonderful grandmothers, Barbara and Joyce

To two loving mothers, Joyanne and Ruthann

To two sweet granddaughters, Emma and Rachel.—JR

To Diane, who found us a yard with a cherry tree.—DC

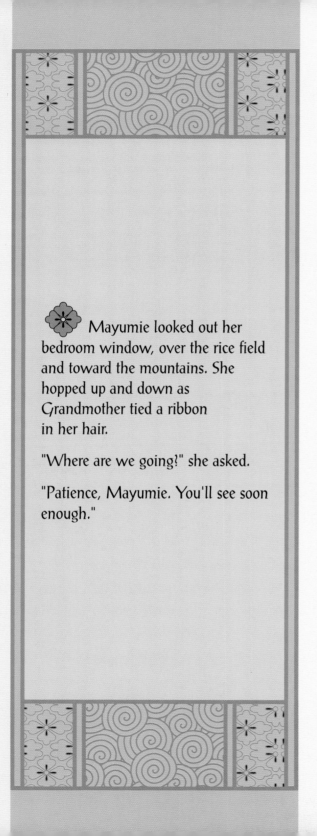 Mayumie looked out her bedroom window, over the rice field and toward the mountains. She hopped up and down as Grandmother tied a ribbon in her hair.

"Where are we going?" she asked.

"Patience, Mayumie. You'll see soon enough."

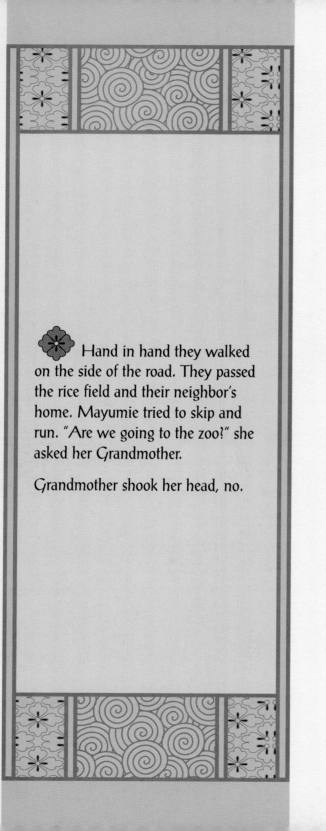

Hand in hand they walked on the side of the road. They passed the rice field and their neighbor's home. Mayumie tried to skip and run. "Are we going to the zoo!" she asked her Grandmother.

Grandmother shook her head, no.

They strolled by the bank and the fruit market to the train station. People pushed and shoved and packed onto the train. Mayumie had to stand. She tried to jump above the people to see out the window. They were too tall. She tried to push them to the side. There were too many.

"Grandmother. Are we going to a museum?" she asked.

Grandmother smiled and quietly said, "No."

 Mayumie hung on to a pole. People swayed back and forth as the train rumbled through the busy towns. *Clickety clack, clickety clack- Kabunk, Kabunk!* It seemed to take forever.

Mayumie caught glimpses of tall buildings through the passengers' heads. "We're going to the city," said Mayumie. "But why!"

"Be patient, Mayumie. We're almost there."

The doors on the train slid open. Mayumie caught hold of Grandmother's hand, and left the train in the river of people.

The city was full of people, lights, cars, steamy streets and familiar smells. *Honk-honk!* sounded car horns. *Beep Beep!* warned mopeds for people to move. *Ding Ding!* rang the bells on bicycles. Mayumie looked all around. "There is the shrine, Grandmother. Are we going there?"

"No, not to the shrine," said Grandmother. "It is more beautiful than a shrine." They kept on walking, Mayumie skipping and hopping to get a better idea of where they were going.

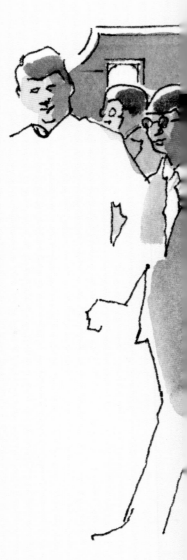

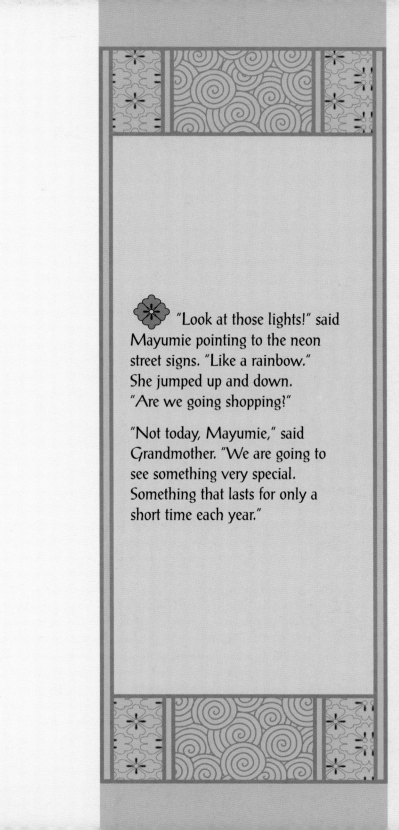

"Look at those lights!" said Mayumie pointing to the neon street signs. "Like a rainbow." She jumped up and down. "Are we going shopping?"

"Not today, Mayumie," said Grandmother. "We are going to see something very special. Something that lasts for only a short time each year."

Mayumie sulked. "We're not going to zoo or a museum or even shopping. Where could we be going!" She stomped her foot on the sidewalk, crossed her arms and refused to move.

"Mayumie. We are almost there. Come with me so you can see." Grandmother walked on slowly but steadily. Mayumie followed.

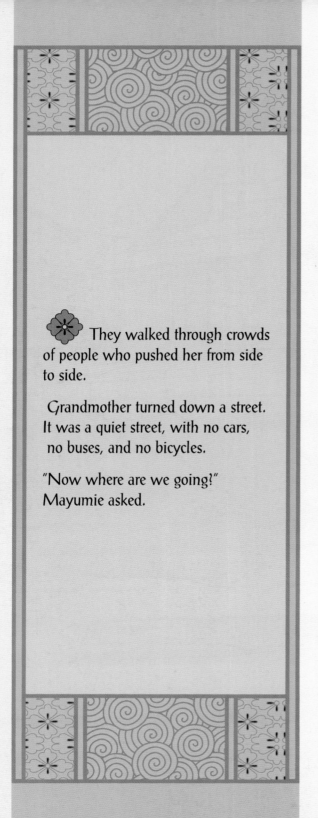

They walked through crowds of people who pushed her from side to side.

Grandmother turned down a street. It was a quiet street, with no cars, no buses, and no bicycles.

"Now where are we going?" Mayumie asked.

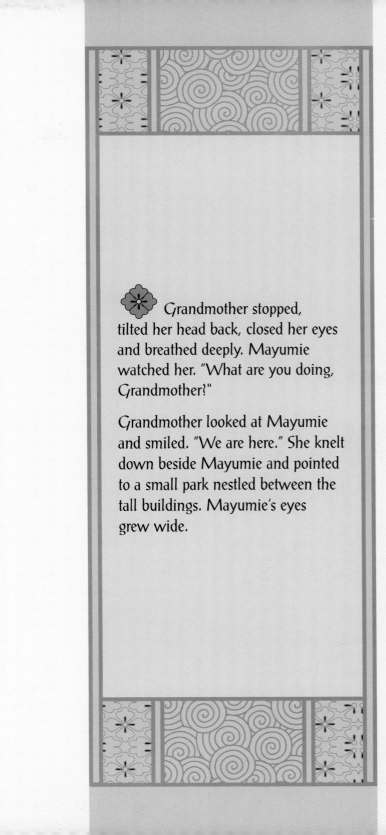

Grandmother stopped, tilted her head back, closed her eyes and breathed deeply. Mayumie watched her. "What are you doing, Grandmother?"

Grandmother looked at Mayumie and smiled. "We are here." She knelt down beside Mayumie and pointed to a small park nestled between the tall buildings. Mayumie's eyes grew wide.

 Rows and rows of trees were covered in pink and white blossoms and looked like big puffy clouds. Every time a breeze swept through the trees, the little blossoms fell gently to the ground. They fell like snow and the ground was blanketed with flowers.

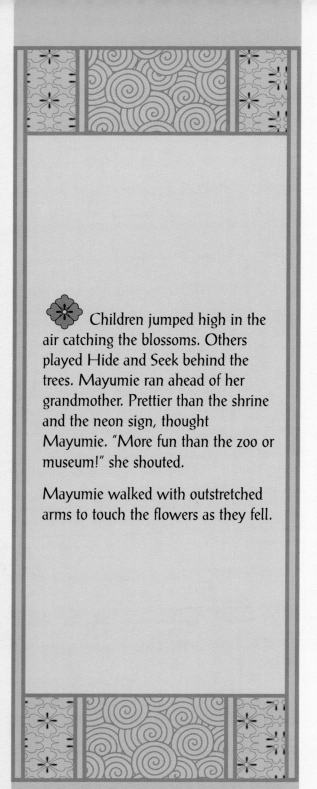

Children jumped high in the air catching the blossoms. Others played Hide and Seek behind the trees. Mayumie ran ahead of her grandmother. Prettier than the shrine and the neon sign, thought Mayumie. "More fun than the zoo or museum!" she shouted.

Mayumie walked with outstretched arms to touch the flowers as they fell.

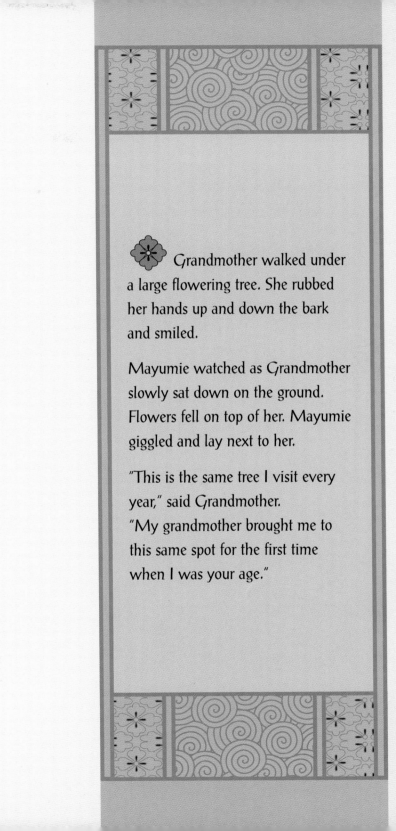

Grandmother walked under a large flowering tree. She rubbed her hands up and down the bark and smiled.

Mayumie watched as Grandmother slowly sat down on the ground. Flowers fell on top of her. Mayumie giggled and lay next to her.

"This is the same tree I visit every year," said Grandmother. "My grandmother brought me to this same spot for the first time when I was your age."

 Mayumie watched the flowers fall and land on her feet. She swept up a handful of flowers, rubbed her nose in the soft petals, and flung the blossoms into the air. The flowers landed on Grandmother's white hair.

"You look like a flower fairy," said Mayumie. "Thank you, Grandmother, for my surprise."

"You are welcome. And next year, we will return at the same time and sit under the same tree."

"Will it still be here next year?" asked Mayumie, looking up through the branches of pink and white petals.

"Yes." Grandmother smiled.

"And we can play in the flowers?"

"Yes," said Grandmother.

"Good." Mayumie watched the flowers fall from the trees.

When they arrived home, Mayumie peered out her window that overlooked the rice fields and gray mountains. She reached in her pocket and pulled out a handful of cherry blossoms. She lined them up on her windowsill. They were starting to turn brown.

"I can visit the zoo or go shopping anytime, but I can only visit you once a year," she said twirling a blossom in her fingers. She lay down on her futon and dreamed about the falling flowers.

Author's Notes:
The Falling Flowers - Jennifer Reed

Pink and white blossoms

A blanket for the cold ground

Spring has now arrived.

Each spring, the Japanese people celebrate the arrival of spring with a flower-viewing party called Hanami. Hana means flower in Japanese. The Cherry Tree Festival is an annual event and many people enjoy the festivities. Young girls and women wear their favorite kimonos. A kimono is a long, silk robe which wraps around your body like a bath robe. Kimonos are worn only for special occasions, but in the past, they were worn all the time. Many kimonos today have cherry blossom prints on them.

The Japanese cherry tree is the symbol and national flower of Japan. The blooms last for only a week. Unlike other cherry trees, they do not yield fruit. They bloom in the spring, grow lush green leaves throughout the summer and come fall, the leaves fall off leaving a bare tree.

Flowering Japanese cherry trees are grown in the United States. In 1912, the city of Tokyo gave the city of Washington D.C. 3020 cherry trees as a gift. The trees are located at the Tidal Basin and around the Jefferson Memorial. People come from all over to enjoy these trees and admire their beauty. The best time to see the trees is late March or early April. They bloom during this time and the flowers last for only two weeks. Residents and visitors of Washington D.C. celebrate the blooming of the cherry trees by holding an annual Cherry Tree Festival, just as they do in Japan. There are many activities, food tasting exhibits and a parade.